This book belongs to

Keiara D. King

Published by Advance Publishers
© 1998 Disney Enterprises, Inc.
All rights reserved. Printed in the United States.
No part of this book may be reproduced or copied in any form
without the written permission of the copyright owner.

Written by Ronald Kidd
Illustrated by Peter Emslie and Niall Harding
Produced by Bumpy Slide Books

ISBN: 1-57973-004-3

10 9 8 7 6 5 4 3 2 1

Walt Disney's Cinderella

THE RUNAWAY WAND

It was the morning after the ball, and Cinderella was dreaming. It was a wonderful dream, filled with music and laughter and dancers gliding across a ballroom floor.

One of the dancers was especially handsome.
As he turned toward Cinderella, she saw that it
was the Prince. He smiled and held out his hand.
"Cinderelly!" he squeaked.

Cinderella opened her eyes. There, perched on the bed, was her friend Jaq the mouse. It was his job to wake her up early each day so she could do her morning chores.

"Sorry t' botheree, Cinderelly," he chattered. "Rook so happy!"

"Yeh," sighed Gus, who was right behind him.
"Happy, happy."

"It's all right," said Cinderella. "You were just
doing your job. Besides, every dream has to end
sometime."

Cinderella climbed out of bed, and the mice and birds brought out her clothes. She sang a tune as she put on the clothes, then went down to clean the courtyard and scrub the floors.

Jaq and Gus, meanwhile, went to take a morning bath in the fountain.

"Zuk-zuk, Gus!" Jaq said. "Over by bench — big sparkly thing!"

Gus perked up. "Pretty, pretty!"

The two mice scurried over to investigate. There, beside the bench, was the Fairy Godmother's magic wand, left behind the night before.

Gus hopped up and down with excitement. "Zuk-zuk! Magic! Ret's do tricks!"

"Don't know, Gus-Gus," Jaq replied. "Wand not ours. Need to ask permission."

"Permission?" asked Gus. "What permission?"

Jaq explained. "When somethin' belong to someone else, need to ask permission to use."

"This wand belong to nice lady last night," said
Gus. "What words she say? Beebbidi-barbidi-bam?"
Jaq laughed. "Bibbidi-bobbidi-boo!"
As he spoke, the magic wand started to glow.

The air shimmered around them, and suddenly, where Jaq and Gus had stood just a moment before, two coach horses pawed the ground!

The horses looked for the coach they had pulled the night before. But there was no coach in sight, so they set off through the fields to explore.

Jaq and Gus raced across the countryside, enjoying their newfound size and speed. They leaped fences, swam rivers, and climbed hills.

They grazed in the grass, but soon they grew tired of adventure and headed home to look for their friend Cinderella.

They found her sweeping the courtyard, and galloped over to greet her. But, not used to being so big, they bumped into trellises and knocked over flowerpots. Before they knew it, the courtyard was a mess.

Cinderella, of course, didn't recognize her friends. All she saw was that she now had more work ahead of her.

"Please, go!" she told the horses. "Shoo!" She waved her broom at them, and Gus and Jaq fled.

Jaq and Gus retreated to the garden, this time being careful not to bump into anything. Looking around, Jaq saw the magic wand lying in the grass. Leaning over, he picked it up carefully in his mouth. As he did, the wand began to quiver and rattle against his teeth.

Jaq let out a frightened whinny and dropped the wand. By the time it hit the ground, his whinny had become a buzz. The two horses had turned into bees!

Delighted to be flying, Jaq flitted through the garden, taking in all the wonderful sights and smells. Suddenly he stopped. What had happened to Gus?

Jaq buzzed back among the flowers, looking for his friend. Finally, at the very edge of the garden, he saw a chubby bee clinging to the face of a giant sunflower, eating great chunks of pollen. It was Gus.

From an open window came the screechy voice of Anastasia, one of Cinderella's wicked stepsisters.

Gus and Jaq grinned at each other and took off flying toward the house.

They buzzed through a second-story window and found Anastasia lounging in bed.

"Cinderella," Drizella yelled from next door, "how are we supposed to get up when you haven't brought our breakfast yet?"

Jaq and Gus flew high above the beds and
began diving at Anastasia. "Bees!" she shrieked.
"I hate bees!"
Jumping from beneath the covers, she raced to

her sister's room with Jaq and Gus buzzing happily along behind. The two sisters ran about frantically, crashing into furniture and knocking pictures off the wall.

When Cinderella arrived a moment later,
Drizella swatted at the air, screaming, "Get rid
of these nasty pests — and clean up this mess!"
Then the sisters ran from the room and slammed
the door, leaving Cinderella alone with the bees.

Cinderella turned to the bees. "Well, you're awfully cute," she said, "but you've caused me a lot of trouble." With that, she shooed them outside and closed the window behind them.

The bees buzzed back to the garden and landed
by the magic wand. Before they knew it, Jaq and
Gus had changed once again. And this time they
had turned into — bulldogs!

Jaq and Gus circled the garden, looking for something a bulldog might like to do. They spied Lucifer the cat, sunning himself on the garden wall.

Barking gleefully, they charged Lucifer. For once, the big, lazy cat moved quickly. He leaped from the wall and ran into the cellar, with Jaq and Gus snapping at his heels.

They chased Lucifer through a pile of ashes, then up the stairs and into the house. Lucifer and the bulldogs raced from room to room, leaving black pawprints wherever they went.

They ran into the parlor, where Cinderella had
just finished scrubbing the floor. Screeching with
fear, Lucifer threw himself into Cinderella's arms,
upsetting her bucket and knocking her over.

"Now look what you've done!" said Cinderella. "Get out! Get out, you mean old dogs!"

Jaq and Gus tried to explain, but all they could manage were pathetic whimpers. Finally they crept outside, their tails drooping.

Cinderella went through the house, taking stock
of the damage. There were pawprints everywhere.
Her stepsisters' rooms were a wreck. And the
courtyard might never be the same. Overcome with
despair, she went to the garden and began to cry.

"Can I help, dear?" asked a kindly voice.

Cinderella turned around, and there was her

Fairy Godmother.

"Oh, Fairy Godmother, it's all so hopeless," she said, dabbing her eyes. Cinderella described what had happened, and the Fairy Godmother nodded sadly.

"I'm afraid it's been a bad day for me, too," she said. "I seem to have lost my magic wand."

The two bulldogs came crawling out from behind the bushes, carrying the magic wand. They dropped it in front of the Fairy Godmother.

"It's those awful dogs!" exclaimed Cinderella.

The Fairy Godmother scratched her chin. "Hmm. I wonder . . ." Lifting the wand, she waved it, saying, "Bibbidi-bobbidi-boo!"

The air sparkled, and suddenly the bulldogs
turned back into mice.

"Jaq and Gus!" said Cinderella. "That was you?"

Jaq nodded unhappily. "Horses, too," he said.
"And bees. Sorry we make mess, Cinderelly."

"You know," said the Fairy Godmother, "I might have let you use the wand if only you had asked permission."

Jaq brightened. "Permission? Really? How 'bout we try one more time? We could fix things."

"What's the magic word?" asked the Fairy
Godmother.
　　"Bibbidi-bobbidi-boo!" said Jaq.
　　"Not this time," she replied. "Guess again."
　　Gus hopped up and down. "Zuk-zuk!" he cried.
"Magic word . . . please!"

The magic wand trembled, and a ball of light appeared over their heads. It swept out of the garden, across the courtyard, through the window, into the bedroom, and all around the house, cleaning as it went. Soon all the mess was gone.

"Wow!" squealed Jaq. "Magic!"

If you have a magic wand,
Here's what you have to do:
Make a wish and say the words,
"Bibbidi-bobbidi-boo!"
But to ask permission,
Here's all you'll ever need —
The little phrase "Please, may I?"
'Cause it's magical, indeed!